MR. MEN LITTLE MISS™

MR. STUBBORN SAYS THERE ARE NO MONSTERS IN THIS BOOK

www.mrmen.com

The publisher does not have any control over and does not assume any responsibility for author or third-party websites or their content.

ISBN 978-0-8431-3581-7   10 9 8 7 6 5 4 3 2 1

PSS!
PRICE STERN SLOAN
www.penguin.com/youngreaders

When it comes to the things that go bump in the night, Mr. Stubborn shows no fear—but that's because he doesn't believe in monsters! These three stories show just how stubborn Mr. Stubborn can be. Even when he is face-to-face with a scary creature, he still refuses to admit he's wrong!

Mr. Stubborn, Mr. Noisy, and Little Miss Naughty wandered through a dark cavern. They were looking for a monster called the Fangasaurus.

"We've been down here for hours and still haven't seen the Fangasaurus. It does not exist!" said Mr. Stubborn.

"I *know* it's real!" protested Little Miss Naughty. "It's *got* to be here."

Mr. Noisy looked around. "What does the map say?" he asked.

Mr. Stubborn unfolded the map. "It says: 'Ignore me and listen to Mr. Stubborn! He knows his way around caves.'" Mr. Stubborn always thought he was right.

Suddenly Little Miss Naughty screamed. "Look! There it is!"
"What? Where?" Mr. Noisy and Mr. Stubborn shouted.
"Ha, ha!" Little Miss Naughty laughed. "Made you look!"
"No more jokes, Little Miss Naughty! Let's move on," said Mr. Stubborn.

"The map says to turn right at the stalagmite," Mr. Noisy shouted. "There it is!"

"That's not a stalagmite. That's a stalac*tite*," argued Mr. Stubborn.

But Mr. Noisy knew how to tell them apart. "Stalac*tites* hang from the ceiling, like that one!" he yelled, pointing up.

"No, you are wrong." Mr. Stubborn insisted. "This is a stalac*tite* on the ground." Mr. Stubborn didn't really know the difference, but he was still sure he was right.

"And *that* is a Fangasaurus!" shrieked Little Miss Naughty.
"Aaaaah!" Mr. Noisy shouted.

"Oops!" giggled Little Miss Naughty. "Sorry, it's just a stalagmite."
"I'm finished looking for your fake monster," said Mr. Stubborn.

Mr. Stubborn set off farther into the cave.

"Um, Mr. Stubborn?" Mr. Noisy hollered after him. "I think this is the way back. Our footprints are coming from *this* direction."

"Those are not footprints. Those are just foot-shaped holes in the dirt," argued Mr. Stubborn.

Suddenly Little Miss Naughty heard a noise. She turned around and came face-to-face with the dreaded Fangasaurus! He picked her up by her hat and tossed her from side to side.

"Mr. Stubborn!" Little Miss Naughty cried. "Mr. Noisy! It's ... it's ..."

"We are done playing your silly games, Little Miss Naughty!" Mr. Stubborn replied, without bothering to look. "I'm telling you, Mr. Noisy, it's this way!"

"I'm calling for help," Mr. Noisy yelled. He sounded the alarm on his megaphone, which was even louder than Mr. Noisy himself!

Startled by Mr. Noisy's siren, the Fangasaurus dropped Little Miss Naughty. Then he ran off, straight through the wall of the cave!

"There's the exit!" cried Mr. Stubborn, spying the monster-shaped hole in the wall. "I knew it was this way! Come on, Little Miss Naughty. I told you there was no monster."

It was Friday the thirteenth and Mr. Stubborn and Little Miss Chatterbox were having dinner at the Dillydale Restaurant.

"Oh my gosh! Look, Mr. Stubborn," said Little Miss Chatterbox. "A full moon! Do you know what happens when there's a full moon on Friday the thirteenth? Somebody's going to turn into a werewolf!"

"There is no such thing as a werewolf," said Mr. Stubborn.
"Oh, but it's true," said Little Miss Chatterbox. "I saw it on TV!"
"You can't believe everything you see on TV!" Mr. Stubborn replied.

Suddenly Mr. Stubborn's ears began to grow bigger. And his nose began to grow longer. He was turning into a werewolf! "I tell you, Little Miss Chatterbox, there is *no such thing* as a werewolf!" Mr. Stubborn said, unaware of the change.

"But Mr. Stubborn," protested Little Miss Chatterbox.

"No. I am right!" said Mr. Stubborn.

"But you just turned *into* a werewolf!" Little Miss Chatterbox yelled.

Mr. Stubborn reached up and touched his werewolf face. "My face has not changed," he insisted.

Just then Mr. Tickle walked up to the table. "Hi, Little Miss Chatterbox. Hi, Mr.—AARGH!" Mr. Tickle screamed, jumping into the air. "Mr. Stubborn, you're a werewolf!"

"I have had enough of this ridiculous talk," said Mr. Stubborn. "There is no such thing as a werewolf!"

But as he walked through the restaurant, everyone screamed in fright.
"AAAH!" bellowed Mr. Noisy as he jumped onto his table.
"Werewolf!" Little Miss Helpful yelped.

Only Little Miss Sunshine remained calm. Mr. Stubborn stopped in front of her table and she held up a mirror.

Mr. Stubborn gazed at his werewolf face, but he refused to admit he was wrong. "This mirror doesn't work," he shouted. "There is no such thing as a werewolf!"

And with that, the werewolf stormed away.

One dark and spooky night, Mr. Stubborn, Mr. Quiet, and Mr. Grumpy walked through the Dillydale Swamp. They were looking for the Dillydale Swamp Monster.

"I'm telling you, gentlemen, it's here somewhere," said Mr. Grumpy.

"This is a waste of time," said Mr. Stubborn. "The Swamp Monster does not exist."

Mr. Grumpy shined his flashlight on his boat. "Look! The monster bit off my motor last night."

"Oooh, that's a big bite," whispered Mr. Quiet.

"Your boat is just cheap! The motor probably fell off on its own," argued Mr. Stubborn.

"But I saw it! I'll prove it to you," said Mr. Grumpy. He pointed to the bucket Mr. Quiet was holding. "Toss that monster bait into the water."

"Gross," muttered Mr. Quiet as he dumped the bait into the swamp.

"Shh. The swamp monster won't come out if there's noise," Mr. Grumpy whispered.

"It won't come out because it does not *exist*!" yelled Mr. Stubborn. "Maybe you saw a frog."

"It was *not* a frog," said Mr. Grumpy.

"Or a turtle," Mr. Stubborn insisted.

"No, it wasn't a turtle, either." Mr. Grumpy rolled his eyes.

Mr. Stubborn shook his flashlight in Mr. Grumpy's face. "I'll bet it was a duck!"

"It was *not* a *duck*!" screamed Mr. Grumpy.

As the two fought, Mr. Quiet peered into the water at two big, black eyes. "Uh, Mr. Grumpy? Mr. Stubborn?" Mr. Quiet whispered. "Definitely not a duck."

The Swamp Monster rose slowly from the water. Mr. Quiet shook in fear. "Um, guys? Monster . . ."

Suddenly the monster's big, sticky, pink tongue shot out and grabbed Mr. Quiet's bucket of bait!

"Um, guys?" Mr. Quiet said again.

"Don't interrupt, Mr. Quiet!" said Mr. Grumpy. "We're having a discussion."

"More like someone who's completely right talking to someone who's completely wrong," yelled Mr. Stubborn.

Just then a giant green hand reached down and plucked Mr. Stubborn off the dock!

The Swamp Monster slowly sank into the water with Mr. Stubborn. Mr. Grumpy didn't even notice! But Mr. Quiet did.

"It's been nice knowing you, Mr. Stubborn," he said as they continued to sink.

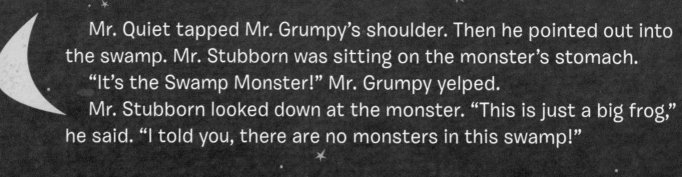

Mr. Quiet tapped Mr. Grumpy's shoulder. Then he pointed out into the swamp. Mr. Stubborn was sitting on the monster's stomach.

"It's the Swamp Monster!" Mr. Grumpy yelped.

Mr. Stubborn looked down at the monster. "This is just a big frog," he said. "I told you, there are no monsters in this swamp!"